Dear Matin,
Hope you enjoy th
Australian books.
♡ your cousins, Dominic + Noah.

Ted Prior

Grug

For Dougal, Lucy and Eve

GRUG AND THE RAINBOW

Published in Australia and New Zealand in 2009 by Simon & Schuster (Australia) Pty Limited
Suite 19A, Level 1, Building C, 450 Miller Street, Cammeray NSW 2062

A CBS Company
Sydney · New York · London · Toronto

Visit our website at www.simonandschuster.com.au

National Library of Australia Cataloguing-in-Publication entry

Author:	Prior, Ted.
Title:	Grug and the rainbow / Ted Prior.
ISBN:	9780731813902 (pbk.)
Series:	Prior, Ted. Grug.
Target Audience:	For children.
Dewey Number:	A823.3

Cover and internal design: Xou Creative
Printed in China: Phoenix Offset

The paper used to produce this book is a natural, recyclable product made from wood grown in sustainable plantation forests. The manufacturing processes conform to the environmental regulations in the country of origin.

10 9 8 7 6 5

Ted Prior

Grug

and the rainbow

SIMON & SCHUSTER
AUSTRALIA A CBS COMPANY

The sky turned dark.

It began to rain. Grug hurried inside …

… to sit in front of his warm cosy fire.

When the rain stopped and the sun came out, Grug sloshed through the wet grass.

He looked up and was surprised to see beautiful coloured stripes across the sky.

Grug went for a closer look ...

... but the stripes moved away.

He tried sneaking up on them.

He tried running after them …

… but the stripes moved even further away.

Then Grug knew what he could do.

He worked hard sawing, hammering ...

... and painting.
At last he had made ...

... his very own rainbow!

Grug

 Grug at
the beach

 Grug and his
bicycle

 Grug and the
big red apple

 Grug builds
a boat

 Grug builds
a car

 Grug and his
garden

 Grug goes
fishing

 Grug goes
to school

 Grug and the
green paint

 Grug has a
birthday

 Grug and
his kite

 Grug learns
to cook

 Grug learns
to dance

 Grug learns
to swim

 Grug meets
Snoot

 Grug and
his music

 Grug in the
playground

 Grug plays
cricket

 Grug plays
soccer

 Grug and the
rainbow

 Grug goes
shopping

 Grug at
the snow

 Grug at
the zoo